This ELMER book belongs to:

. . . .

For Blake

This paperback edition first published in 2013 by Andersen Press Ltd.
First published in Great Britain in 2008 by Andersen Press Ltd.,
20 Vauxhall Bridge Road, London SW1V 2SA.
Published in Australia by Random House Australia Pty.,
Level 3, 100 Pacific Highway, North Sydney, NSW 2060.
Copyright © David McKee, 2008
The rights of David McKee to be identified as the author and illustrator
of this work have been asserted by him in accordance with
the Copyright, Designs and Patents Act, 1988.
All rights reserved.
Colour separated in Switzerland by Photolitho AG, Zürich.
Printed and bound in Singapore by Tien Wah Press.

10   9   8   7   6   5   4   3   2   1

British Library Cataloguing in Publication Data available.

ISBN 978 1 84270 759 3

This book has been printed on acid-free paper

ELMER
and the BIG BIRD

David McKee

Andersen Press

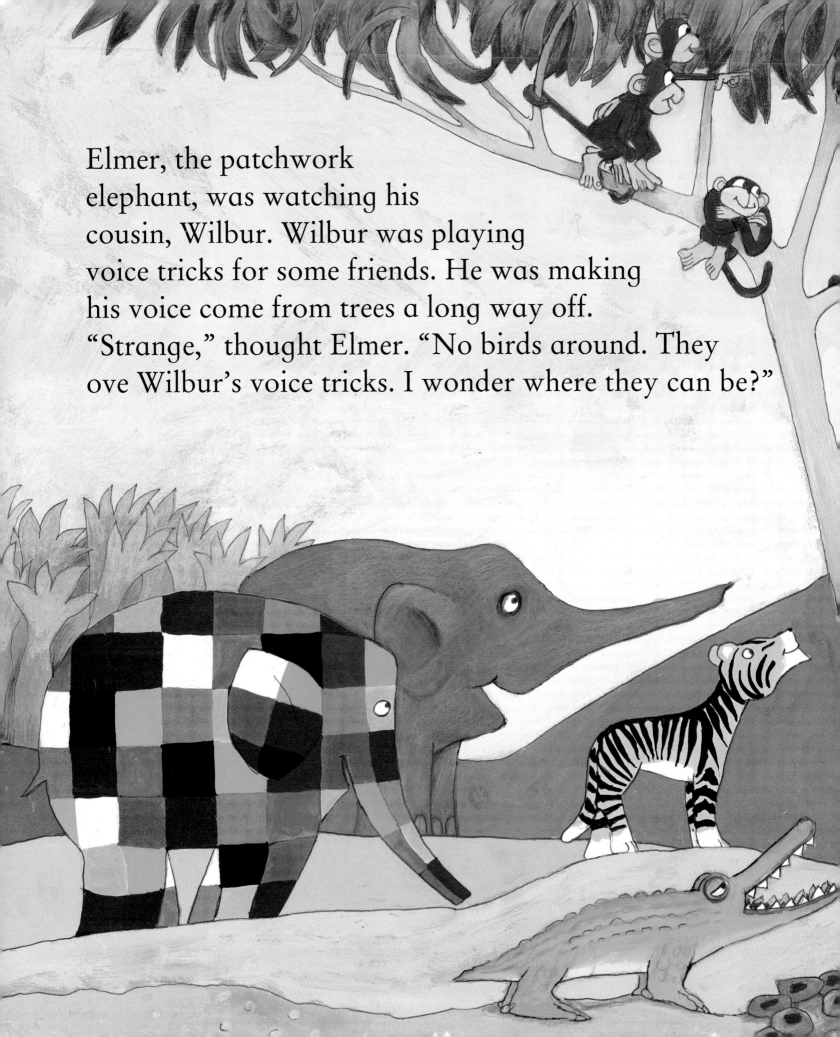

Elmer, the patchwork
elephant, was watching his
cousin, Wilbur. Wilbur was playing
voice tricks for some friends. He was making
his voice come from trees a long way off.
"Strange," thought Elmer. "No birds around. They
ove Wilbur's voice tricks. I wonder where they can be?"

Elmer left the others and went to find the birds. As he walked, he called out, "Yo ho, birds. Where are you?" Suddenly a bird flew out of a cave and said, "Shh, Elmer! Quickly! Come inside."

The cave was full of birds.

"We're hiding from that huge, nasty, bully bird that's on the red rock," said one. "He frightens us. Have you seen him?"
"No," said Elmer. "I'll go and talk to him."
"That won't do any good," sighed a bird as Elmer left.

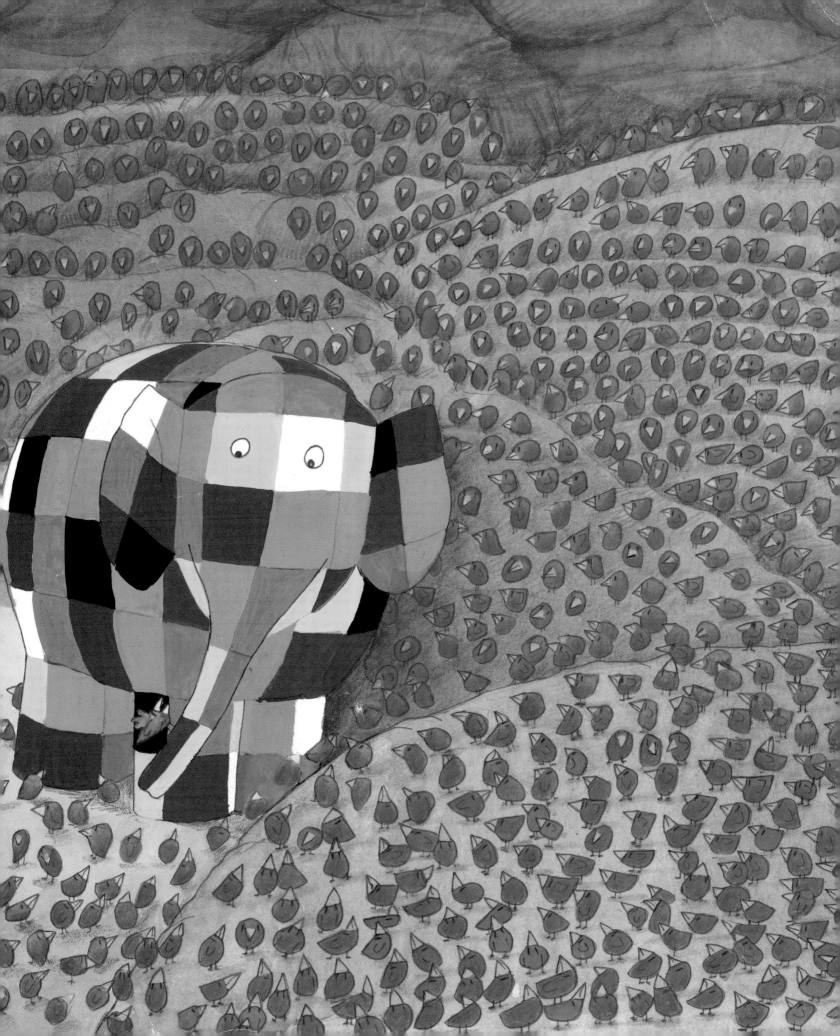

Sure enough, there was a big bird on the rock. "Hello, you're new here," said Elmer. "You're welcome to stay but, please, don't frighten the little birds."
"Frighten them? They'll do as I say, or I'll do more than frighten them!" screeched the bird. "I like to frighten, and I'll decide if I stay or not!"

Elmer returned to Wilbur and the others and told them about the bully bird. "If he won't stop being nasty," said Elmer, "I'll need your help and the help of the really big bird."

"The really big bird?" asked Wilbur.

"Yes," said Elmer. "Here's the plan."

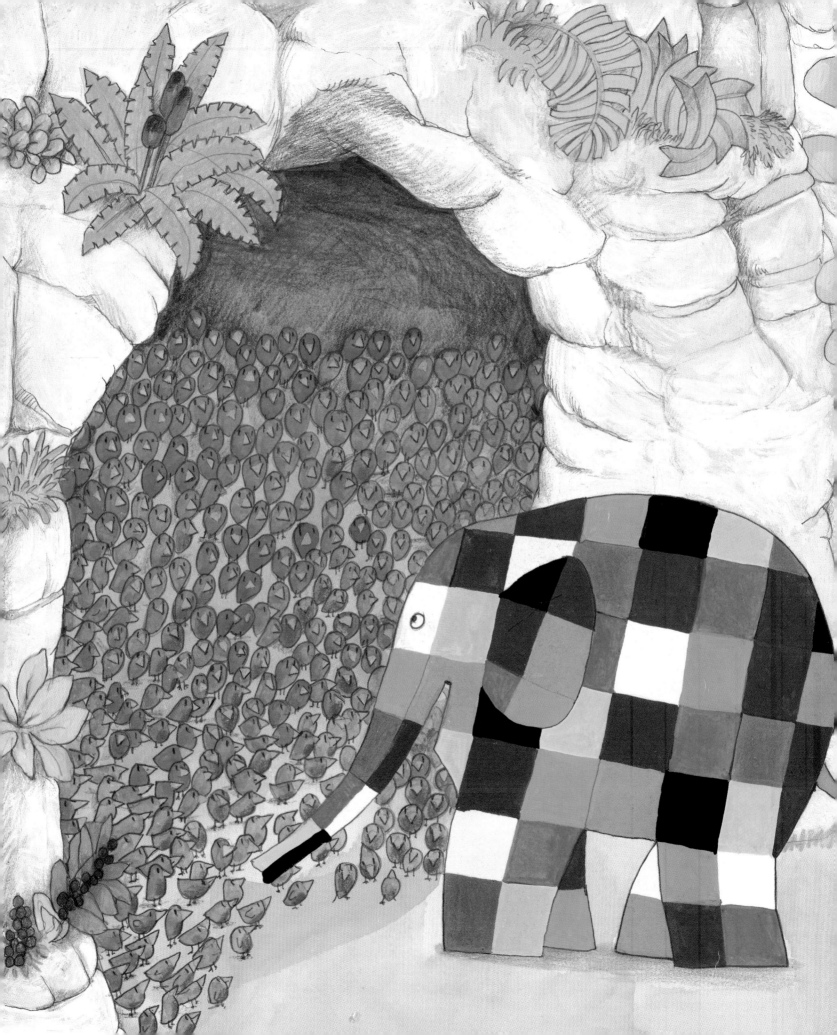

Next Elmer went back to the birds and said, "You're right, the bully is awful. We might need the really big bird."
"The really big bird?" asked the little birds in chorus.
"Yes," said Elmer. He explained what he intended to do, and then said, "That bully gets one more chance. If he's still nasty, I'll call the really big bird."

The bully bird saw Elmer coming. "Stupid elephant," he muttered. "I'll scare him." He dived straight at Elmer. Elmer hummed a little tune and pretended not to notice. The bird hurtled down, screamed and, at the last minute, swooped up again to his rock. Elmer acted as if nothing had happened.

"Are you all right?" Elmer asked. "You sounded frightened."

"Frightened? Me?" scoffed the bully bird. "Fat chance."

"Well," said Elmer. "The birds have a friend much bigger than you. Leave them in peace or I'll call him."
"Bigger than me? Impossible!" shrieked the bully bird. "Leave them in peace indeed. Call him. Go on, call him!"
Elmer trumpeted loudly. A deep voice came from far away.
"Where's the horrible bully who frightens little birds?"
In the distance, something started to rise.

At that moment there was the sound of running and the animals came racing by. "Run for it, Elmer," they called. "The really big bird is coming!"

"He . . . he can't be that big," stammered the bully bird.

The rising shape was an enormous bird. "Let's see what a really nasty bird can do," came the voice.
"Oh no! I've just remembered," said the bully bird. "It's Uncle's birthday. I must go." He left very quickly.
"Come back! Coward!" called the voice. But the bully bird had gone.

The huge bird came closer, changed shape and started to break up. It wasn't one bird, it was all the small birds flying closely together! Laughing happily, they began to land. Wilbur came out of hiding as the animals returned. "Well done, everybody," said Elmer. "I loved the voice, Wilbur!"

"Thank you, all," said one of the small birds. "Now we can live normally again."
From the distance came the voice of the really big bird. "That's what I call togetherness."
Elmer laughed. "Thank you, Wilbur. I couldn't have put it better myself."